THE HALLOWEEN BET

ABBY KNOX

This book is dedicated to Luke Danes. If you know who that is, then we can be friends.

The Halloween Bet

By Abby Knox

Dive bartender Blake Pritchard has zero interest in joining in the silliness of his town's Fall Festival, including a new ghost tour of a house that's definitely not haunted.

Blake's ex girlfriend and local historian Dahlia Jordan is determined to get Blake into the spirit, and bets him that he won't last one night at the haunted house without getting properly spooked.

This is a very quick and sexy stand alone short read with a second chance theme, an HEA, and no cheating. Also contains a dunk tank, some pound cake, a possibly haunted house, dubious points of interest, and other shenanigans along the way as these two crazy kids work things out and finally get back together!

Chapter One

Here she comes, her festive orange pumps clip-clopping down the sidewalk, headed straight into my bar.

Shit.

Any notion I had of escaping participation in the town-wide Halloween-gasm that is this year's Harvest Festival blows out the door as soon as Dahlia Jordan, Tourism Director, blows in.

Her golden eyes sparkle and her perpetual smile broadens when she spots me behind the bar. It's a smile so genuine, I almost feel an old, familiar twinge.

But then I remember she's not coming in for a friendly drink after work. It's noon on Halloween and her office is closed today. But under her relentless guidance, downtown is decked out in black cats and spiderwebs, and every food establishment is serving something pumpkin flavored.

The way she's walking, I can tell she needs something.

Oh, Dahlia doesn't need me personally; she needs something from me as the proprietor of the Southpaw Tavern. She'd better not be coming in here trying to convince me to serve pumpkin ale, because it ain't happening.

Along with the gust of October air she pulls in with her comes her warm caramel apple pie scent, heavy on the cinnamon. Same as it was back when I had permission to take a whiff of her hair freely and on the regular. Same damn sweet energy as always, as if life has never broken her down.

In the two years since Dahlia and I broke up, she's grown into herself. Me, I've been knocked around a bit. I lost my Gramps who raised me, inherited his bar, had to pay off his back taxes, and I'm still working on paying down a mountain of the business's debt. Unlike me, the old man was a sweetheart who let a bunch of local barflies run up ridiculous tabs. Even if Gramps had known he would die of a sudden heart attack at the age of 65, I doubt he would have tried to collect the money some of those patrons owed him.

What is Dahlia doing back in this town, anyway? I've been asking myself that for the past six months, ever since she moved back home to take over the tourism office. I thought she'd be busy slaying every eligible bachelor in the big city by now.

Any man without his wits about him would fall all over himself to please this auburn-haired bombshell with the glowing skin and glossy lips.

But I do have my wits about me. I'm Blake Fuckin' Pritchard, after all—the only bartender still serving cheap domestic beer in this up-and-coming little town. My bar doesn't have Wi-Fi. I program the jukebox myself and fuck you if you don't like it. Bouncing unruly customers with my own hands gives me joy. People fear me, and I like it that way.

So, I feel confidently immune to Dahlia's charms. This gorgeous creature cannot distract me from the fact that she carries something under her arm—something that can only mean one thing for me: extra work.

"Happy Halloween, Blake! Here's your jack-o'-lantern!" How can someone's voice be both perky and sexy? Doesn't matter. Has no effect on me.

"I didn't order one," I say, focusing on wiping down the oak bar in front of me and not the orange and purple blob she's lifting onto the bar.

She laughs, unaffected by my rotten attitude. "Every downtown business gets a painted jack-o'-lantern. It's part of the game." Dahlia plops the thing down onto the spot I just polished.

I eye her suspiciously as I hand dry a rack of lowball glasses Kenny just pulled from the dishwasher. Dahlia talks with her hands, just like she used to do back when we were an item. The difference now is those hands are professionally manicured, with pictures of tiny ghosts festively adorning her fingernails. In fact, her entire look these days is deliberate and polished. I always liked her makeup-free face and air-dried hair back then. But I have to admit, I'm liking this current look just as much. Not going to say that out loud, though.

"I don't know about any game; ergo, I'm not participating."

Undeterred, she chirps, "Everybody's participating. It's a social media trick-or-treat game, but for grown-ups."

I grunt and say to her, "If it involves me pretending I like tourists, then you can just skedaddle with that pumpkin."

"Blake, come on. You don't have to pretend you like people. It's part of your charm."

I stop wiping down glasses and look at her hard. There's a whole lot more she's not telling me.

I can see I'm not getting rid of her soon so I pour her the

usual—an amaretto sour with a cherry—and set it down in front of her.

She thanks me and sips it. Her lip quirks.

"This is watered down," she says.

I sigh heavily and let my head loll back on my neck, as if the tacky stained-glass Bud Light pendant lamp hanging above the bar will tell me how to win this argument—the same argument we've been having since she moved back here to her hometown. "We've been through this before, Dahlia. No, it's not."

She shrugs. "Tastes watered down."

I huff. "It's on the house, then. I don't know what to tell you, D. It's amaretto, simple syrup, and lemon juice—that's it. If you don't like it, why don't you order a beer instead of a sorority sister drink?"

She frowns, but still manages not to look offended. "I wasn't in a sorority."

I snort. "You order drinks like you are."

"Is this abuse necessary?" she says with a wink.

I come around to the front of the bar to polish the brass rail. I don't want to get closer to her but some of the people who drink here are slobs, and I don't want their fingerprints on the rail. I'm pretty particular about this whole new hand-crafted set-up. As I should be; it was my hands that did the work after my Gramps died and left the bar to me. Gramps, who was one of the most famous left-handed pitchers ever in the American League, retired to this town and lived out the rest of his days slinging drinks. Why? Because he loved talking to people and people loved hearing stories from his glory days. I didn't inherit that extrovert gene. But this place meant a lot to him, so it means everything to me.

"Abuse? You're the one who accused me of watering down my drinks, which I do not do. Maybe your tastes are changing."

"Excuse me?"

I don't really feel like elaborating, but she brings it out of me. "I read an article that says every seven years your taste buds change. Foods that tasted bad to you when you were younger, maybe you like them now. Maybe your favorite thing isn't your favorite anymore."

She leans forward against the bar, engaging us in an odd game of chicken. As I polish the brass rail with a rag, I keep getting closer to her, but she fails to move her body out of my way.

"Excuse me," I say and she moves back, but I'm in such a rush and she's not quick enough, so my bicep grazes her boob.

"Whoops. Sorry," I grunt.

I finish the job while she stares at me, speechless for once in her life.

Neither of us say anything for a few painfully long seconds. Finally, I move on to cleaning the tables that don't need cleaning while she recovers her composure.

Dahlia says, "You do realize you're saying this to someone who is extremely loyal to her own tastes and sensibilities. My taste buds are exactly the same as always."

After whipping the towel into a laundry bin behind the bar and grabbing a clean one from the fresh pile that Kenny brought down from the dryer in my upstairs apartment, I say, "That sounds like a personal problem."

She takes another sip and shrugs. I guess free drinks taste better.

"Back to the subject at hand. You just have to stand there and be your usual self."

I could bounce her for beating around the bush. I've tossed plenty of dude bros out of my bar for lesser offenses, such as wearing Axe body spray. "What are you up to?"

She downs the drink, and her eyes focus on the ceiling to

avoid meeting my gaze for a moment as she gathers up her courage.

"Dahlia."

Her shoulders drop. "Ugh. Fine. You just have to stand there while people take a selfie with you and/or Kenny."

"The fuck are you talking about? I don't do selfies."

But she's in tourism director mode. Winning personality, dauntless enthusiasm. "Everyone who attends the Fall Festival gets a map of all the downtown businesses that have a painted jack-o'-lantern somewhere in their stores. They take a selfie with the proprietor and then post it on social media with the hashtag—"

"Nobody is allowed to say the 'H' word in here. Also I don't have Wi-Fi."

She ignores me and continues. "...With the hashtags printed on the map and they're entered in a drawing. It was Amanda Hall's idea. She's one of my volunteers today so this definitely has to happen."

Fidgeting, I twist my towel around my hand. Mentioning the mayor's wife's name isn't going to help bring me around. The last time the Halls were in my bar, it was to drop weird, indirect hints that I should stop putting in my low-cost construction bids for small parks projects. Screw the Halls.

"Lot of rigmarole to enter a drawing. I'll make it easy for you. Have everyone put their business card in a fishbowl, shake it up..."

"Bo-ring!" she chuckles and dismisses me with a wave of her hand.

That smile of hers could win over an angry Shrek. But it's not working on me. "I like boring. Boring, same old customers pay my light bill. One-time visitors and transient millennial newcomers do not."

"But that's kind of the point. We attract new people, and those people come back and become regulars, improving your bottom line. Also, you are a millennial as much as I am." She points at me, not letting me get away with my rant.

I shake my head. "This bar's bottom line hasn't improved in years and I don't need it to. I didn't inherit this fine establishment and its elite clientele from Gramps," I say, waving my arm toward Sleepy Ernie, passed out in a booth in the corner, "expecting to get rich."

"Is he OK?" Dahlia asks, switching from a winning smile to genuine concern, leaning forward to get a better look at the man in the corner booth.

Nobody ever asks about Sleepy Ernie, but of course Dahlia does.

I wave in his direction. "He works a rotating shift at the plant, and it fucks with his circadian rhythm. This is his after-work drink. He'll wake up in an hour and I'll have a donut for him, then he'll shuffle home to sleep for real."

Dahlia smiles at me with her mouth closed. It's a knowing smile accompanied by a series of rapid blinks. Her face is an emoji with heart eyes.

"What?" I ask.

She squeaks. "You do like people. You take care of Ernie."

"Let's not get carried away."

She continues, "And who said anything about getting rich? Come on, where's your Halloween spirit?"

"I have plenty of Halloween spirit," I say, flailing my arms. I'm losing my patience. "This is the only bar that hands out candy to the downtown trick-or-treaters, and I hand out full-size Reese's. I don't fuck around with *fun size*."

Dahlia cocks her head and gives me big doe eyes. "I'm so glad you have a heart for kids. Because, in other news..." She bites her lip in hesitation.

Shit. I knew I shouldn't have said all that. "Oh god. What now?" I ask, pausing my table polishing to face her, because I can't believe she's asking me for even more help.

"Well...that brings me to my other scheme..."

I nod and cross my arms over my chest. "At least you admit it's a scheme. Go on."

Dahlia ignores my jab and goes on. "Since you're so full of Halloween spirit then you should have no problem whatsoever filling in for Doctor Howard at the dunk tank in five minutes. He usually does it but he has an emergency appendectomy."

I go from nodding to shaking my head in defiance. "No. No fucking way."

Dahlia presses her palms together pleadingly. "Come on, Blake, the town is counting on you."

I turn away and get back to wiping down the table tops. "No, they count on Doctor Howard. Everybody loves him. Nobody is going to pay money to throw a baseball to dunk me"—I thump my chest with my towel-wrapped fist for emphasis"—into a tank full of water."

The cackle that bursts out of her is so loud it's uncalled for. "Plenty—and I mean *plenty*—of people would love to dunk you. And it's for charity."

I rub the scruff on my chin. For what charity would I allow myself to be humiliated, not to mention risk hypothermia?

"How cold is the water?" I ask.

As soon as I say this I know I should not have. "What kind of a man asks that question?" she says, brow furrowed in disappointment.

Not that her opinion of my manhood matters, but I won't have my masculinity called into question. I stare her down with a look that usually sends dude's nuts shrinking up into their body cavities. Dahlia, however, doesn't seem fazed at all.

I scratch my fingertips across my scalp, sending my hair flopping to the side. "If you tell me it's to raise money for the tourism bureau, you can forget it."

She rolls back her shoulders in a huffy, prissy, and adorable way. "As a matter of fact, it's for the children's library. As you know, the city overshot its budget with the construction of the new clock tower, so they had to hold off on renovations to the children's wing of the library. A very generous anonymous donor will match whatever funds we raise to help renovate it."

Well now she's got me. Our little town's library is in dire need of everything. And that stupid clock tower, in my personal opinion, was nothing but a boondoggle.

I slap my towel on a table and gruffly tell Kenny to take over for me.

"Fine. Show me where to go."

Dahlia slips her hand into the crook of my arm—the arm that I hadn't offered.

I don't pull away from her. I should pull away, but I kind of don't want to. We're not a couple. We haven't even discussed our terrible breakup since she moved back here six months ago. All she's done is pester me at my bar and all I've done is give her a superficially hard time while I serve her drinks.

At the moment, though, my body doesn't listen to my mind. My blood pressure and my mutinous cock have at this moment decided they still like her. My body would very much like to give her a different kind of hard time...up against the bar. But that would be a bad idea.

It's just a chemical thing, I tell myself. Or a muscle memory thing. Not a heart thing. If she wants to walk arm in arm, whether just to be friendly or to ward off other dudes, then I'm all about that. Or, maybe she's afraid I might run away. That's not out of the realm of possibility.

As we make our way down the street on this sunny afternoon, I practice my scowl while she chatters away. A few people waiting in line for their corn dogs are staring at us. If

Dahlia's not careful, she's going to make people think we're an item again, walking around arm in arm in front of everyone in town.

Then again, she does this to everybody, as I recall. Dahlia is not only the town cheerleader but she's very touchy with people she's close with. She's one of those comfortable, born-and-raised-here locals who shakes hands for a really long time. Who gently grasps a friend by the shoulder when they make her laugh. So I shouldn't read anything at all into the fact that we're traipsing around with our arms locked together.

We pass by the pumpkin pound cake contest, where about seven cakes total are spread out on a gingham tablecloth, each with a small ballot box for everyone to cast their votes.

"But why pumpkin pound cake? Why not pumpkin pie?" I ask.

She replies as if she's telling me facts and not opinions. "Halloween is about candy and pumpkin-flavored things leading up to the pie months. November and December are the pie months."

"November is tomorrow," I remind her.

"Exactly. Not pie month for another seven hours."

Has this lady become more bonkers since we dated? I steal a curious glance at her as we walk on. Her long hair curls around her shoulders in drapey layers, framing a fine-boned face with plump lips. Huge eyes that dance when she talks about Halloween. She's not cute. She's not beautiful. She is devastating, especially as the afternoon sun casts golden rays across her luminous skin and makes her lips shimmer and her eyes sparkle.

If she wasn't totally bananas about the town, and about dragging me along with her for the ride to Crazyville, I might find her irresistibly kissable. I might find myself wishing she would turn to me and twine those long, curvy legs around my thighs without warning, like she used to do. Two years plus change has done nothing to diminish her overall allure. Objectively speaking.

We stroll past the craft bazaar, where artists are hawking garden gnomes and handmade wreaths, homemade candles and soaps, and hand knit scarves. "After you close up you can come join me on the midnight ghost tour," she says, like that's also something I should know about.

I scoff. "Ghost tour? Come on. This town has no ghosts."

She abruptly stops by a small booth with a bunch of brochures fanned out on the table. She holds one of the leaflets up for me to see.

"Bite your tongue, sir. See?"

"I will do no such thing," I reply. "What are you shoving in my face?"

She shakes it. "This. This ghost. I'll have you know that the tourism bureau just came into ownership of the Milton House and it is definitely haunted. Maybe even two ghosts now that poor Esther died, may she rest in peace."

I'm embarrassed for her. "The what house? You mean the house with the lady who would sic her doberman on us if we so much as sneezed when we rode our bikes past her grass?"

She beams. "That's the one."

I shake my head. "We're calling it 'Milton House' now? It sounds like one of those places with a pretentious plaque from the register of historic places."

"It *is* one of those places!" she retorts.

"Says who?"

"Says the National Register of Historic Places, just as soon as they approve my application."

I have to rub my temples.

"And how many people do you have signed up for this so-called ghost tour?"

She chirps, "None yet, but I just came up with the idea this morning so word hasn't gotten around yet. I think that once people are feeling nice and festive after the scavenger hunt..."

"Drunk," I interject. "You mean after people get drunk."

"...I'm sure to have some takers."

I'm smiling now, but not because I'm at all interested in signing on to this lunacy. "What other stops do you have on this ghost tour?"

She shrugs. "If you're not interested in ghosts, then I'm not going to tell you."

Fine by me, as long as it's not the empty lot down the street where a moldy old inn used to stand, and where the town's more dotty locals insist Abraham Lincoln once slept. I need to stop asking myself why Dahlia moved back here and start asking myself why I stayed.

"Oh, I'm interested, all right," I tell her. "Interested in debunking all the chicanery of so-called ghost tours."

She juts out her luscious bottom lip, like she has no idea what she's tempting me to do to it. "Why do you have to be such a party pooper?"

I consider ending this argument by sucking that pouty lip right into my mouth and licking it until we both forget what we're arguing about. "I'm not a party pooper. I'm a realist. There is no such thing as ghosts."

She clears her throat and thrusts out her chin. Uh oh. I know that move. She's going to try to challenge me to something. Feats of strength, maybe? See if I can toss my shoe clear over the roof of the bar? "Blake, I'll bet you $100 that I can make you a believer."

I snicker. "Hey, let's make it more interesting than money. If you make me believe in ghosts, I will do anything you ask me to do. For the town. In perpetuity."

She stops abruptly and squints up at me. "Even serve on a subcommittee?"

I grit my teeth because that sounds like the most painful punishment anyone could dole out to me. I would rather eat glass than go to a meeting. "I'll do anything you ask," I grit out.

"But how will I know if I've actually convinced you?"

"Am I an honest man?"

"Yes. Brutally honest sometimes."

This comment makes me wince. I know exactly what she's referring to. She's remembering some of the things I said to her when we broke up. In fairness, we were both pretty brutal to each other.

"OK. Then on my honor. And if I can prove to you that it's all a bunch of baloney, I don't have to do any stupid town things ever again."

She surveys me and taps her chin in thought. I take the opportunity to look away from her before I say anything that will make her mad or inadvertently volunteer my services for something else. Some services I would not mind volunteering for, especially if they involved warming her up. That sleeveless black dress she's wearing is totally unsuitable for the weather.

I bite the inside of my cheek as I look around and take in the scope of all the things she made happen today. I have to say, despite it being a bit over the top and a little looney, I'm impressed. She worked hard. The entire town and then some have turned out for this year's Fall Festival, which is more than I can say about years past.

"The thing is, proving or disproving the existence of ghosts could take a lot longer than a one-hour ghost tour," she says.

"Probably true."

"So what do you propose?"

I shrug. "I don't know. I could spend the night?" Whoa.

Did I just say that? The smell of funnel cakes and cotton candy must be going to my head.

"Excuse me?"

"At the supposedly haunted house."

She shakes her head and points in the direction of the hill, atop which sits Milton House. "I can't let you spend the night alone. The lawyers would have a fit. Besides, I haven't physically been inside the house yet, myself. Once we took possession, I changed the locks, but that's all that's been done up there. It could be dangerous."

And then my mouth totally runs away from my brain. "Fine, then you stay in the house with me."

Dahlia cocks her head to one side. "Blake."

Oh, but I've boarded the train and now I have to ride it all the way to Whackjob City. "Don't think of it as a sleepover. It's just friends, making a bet, on Halloween. For science," I say.

She squints at me, like she doesn't quite believe my motivation but is sort of into the idea despite both of us knowing it's a terrible one. "Well, if it's for science. You're on, Blake Pritchard."

We stand there for a second, just looking at each other like a couple of dopes.

"Well, here we are," Dahlia chirps, gesturing toward the row of carnival games in front of us.

"This is ridiculous," I huff, looking at the large dunk tank with a hunk of timber suspended over it that looks barely large enough to sit my ass on.

Her golden eyes are so bright, I feel like they might leave a mark on me. In a way, they already have, but that's old news.

Perceiving my gaze on her as hesitation, she reminds me, "It's for the kids, remember?"

Chapter Two

Dahlia

Blake Pritchard has no idea how cute he is.

Never did. Not even when we used to date.

And now, two years and some later, when he walks away from me, it's an even better view. Too bad the last time he walked away from me I was cussing him out. Not my classiest move.

Blake mounts the steps at the back of the dunk tank and starts to unbutton his flannel shirt.

What I should do now is walk away.

What I should not do is think about the last time we were alone together, and how I helped him unbutton that very same shirt. Because as much fun as we had, all those good memories are intertwined with the feelings of how badly he hurt me. He broke my heart, though I wasn't exactly an innocent party.

And now, he's about to pick at my scabbed-over feelings by taking off all his clothes in front of the whole town.

Wait a minute, why is he taking off all his clothes?

Blake already removed his flannel and undershirt while I was standing there spacing out, and it looks like he's about to undo the fly of his jeans.

I flail my arms to get his attention. "Wait, no. What are you doing?"

He turns to glare at me and it does things to my body. My cheeks turn beet red, an impulse I've trained myself to control—almost—since moving back to town. I had to—his is the only bar that plays decent music and I can't have him thinking I want to get back together with him.

But now, my body doesn't care about my carefully controlled reactions to his bare bicep—the one that grazed my boob accidentally just moments earlier. Or to his broad chest, rippled stomach, muscled back. Oh god. I have to bite my lip to keep from gasping out loud. His bare skin is golden under the autumn sun and shows a glorious layer of fuzz. The way he's glaring at me, my body's reaction is going to get worse in a second.

"This is a family-friendly event. You have to keep your clothes on, Blake, as much as everyone appreciates the view."

He narrows his eyes at me. "I don't want to get my clothes wet."

I shake my head like I'm speaking to an obstinate teenager. "You can change afterward."

Blake is not happy. Not that it's easy to tell when he's happy or mad. He basically has two expressions: mad and annoyed. "It's laundry day. This is my last pair of clean jeans and shirt."

I blink. "You mean you actually have other jeans and shirts? What did you do? Buy a half dozen of the same plaid flannel shirt and change them out?"

"No. I have one in each color."

Another man's voice interrupts us. "If you two are quite finished..."

I turn and I see Mayor Pete Hall thumping a baseball into a well-worn glove on his left hand. Under his arm is tucked a small megaphone, which he used to open the festival earlier today with a super-boring speech about his precious clock tower. It was full of unnecessary compliments toward the builder, Mason Construction.

"Oh! Hi, Mister Mayor," I say. "I see you brought your own baseball to throw out the first pitch!"

Usually fairly gregarious with me, the mayor seems a bit peeved. I can't blame him. It's easy for Blake and me to get caught up in our banter, irrespective of what's going on around us.

"Let's get on with it," he says, "And please tell Mr. Pritchard to get dressed. This is a dunk tank for the kids, not Chippendales."

I grin at Mayor Hall as everyone milling around us laughs at his corny comment.

I turn back to Blake, whose eyes shoot flaming daggers at me as he slips his t-shirt back on and tosses me his flannel.

When I catch it, I get a whiff of booze, brass polish and the signature, undefinable masculine scent of Blake. But there is also something new I'm not expecting: wood shavings. I wonder what that's about. And I wonder why I like it so much. I have to control myself from lifting the shirt to my nose and inhaling him into my lungs. The only reason my eyes don't roll up into my head at his scent is that I also remember that Blake is insufferable and actively dislikes me.

I watch as he seats himself on the wood plank over the water-filled tank. Once he's seated, he looks over at me with a dark expression I can't place.

I walk over and place my palm on the plexiglass of the tank, look up at him, and give him my brightest smile.

"Thank you for doing this, Blake. It shows that underneath your crotchety facade, and despite everything that's happened between us, you're a good egg."

He mutters something, but I don't hear it. I turn around and ask the mayor if I may borrow the megaphone.

"If I may have everyone's attention! Blake Pritchard is in the dunk tank. I repeat! Pay a dollar and get your revenge on Blake Pritchard. All for a good cause! Come on, everyone! How many of you haven't wanted to throw a baseball at the guy who waters down your drinks?"

"Hey!" I hear Blake say. "I don't water down my drinks!"

I am on a roll. "How many of you have been tossed out of the Southpaw for asking for a Wi-Fi password? Or for wearing a flat-brimmed ball cap? Or asking for a craft beer? Or asking to turn on a game he's not interested in? I know a lot of you want to watch this sorry son of a biscuit eater get wet!"

By the time I'm done having my say, the dunk tank line stretches all the way back to the craft bazaar.

I think my job here is done for now. I hand the megaphone back to the mayor and turn to give Blake a wink and a thumbs up.

"Hey! P.T. Barnum. How long am I expected to..."

Blake doesn't get to finish that sentence, as the mayor's baseball nails the target on the first try.

Judging by the audience's reaction, Dunk-a-Blake is going to raise a boatload of money for the children's library.

I have to go check on a few other things, but I turn back for a second to take a last peek. The now very wet bartender is mounting the little plank again, looking mad as hell. I can hear him using his anger to egg on everyone in line.

This makes me happy. Yes, he was a good choice. The perfect choice.

Chapter Three

Blake

Even though I had the foresight to remove my shoes before I got soaking wet, my jeans are dripping into my shoes so they still make an embarrassing squelchy sound as I make my way down the midway, looking for Dahlia. I should have made that woman go and fetch me dry clothes from somewhere, in exchange for doing her this favor.

People stare and snicker at me. I don't care; I just want my shirt back. And then I want to go home, dry off, get back to the bar and toss that damn jack-o'-lantern in the trash.

I find Dahlia sitting alone at the information booth for the ghost tour. She doesn't see me coming yet because she's busy chatting with some folks and handing out fliers.

Something about her, something about the way she is the complete opposite way that I am around people—vulnerable and pure—makes me smile on the inside. She is always on. Always smiling, always looking like she's ready to have fun. Gramps was the same way; it makes sense that he liked her so much. I can understand why Gramps was sad about my breakup with Dahlia. I watch people around her and it's clear to me she makes everyone around her happy. Nobody leaves her booth without a smile on their face.

I haven't felt an easiness like that in over two years.

A fleeting thought occurs to me: she'd probably raise a hell of a lot more money if she'd just open a kissing booth instead, as it looks like every guy within ten miles is hanging around her booth just to talk to her.

Wait a minute. What am I thinking? I don't want anyone kissing her. Especially not guys like the ones staring at her from just feet away at the ring toss game. A couple of dude bros with too much money and too much time on their hands are both checking her out and making comments to each other. And it looks as if their girlfriends are standing not five feet away.

But what do I care what she gets up to, or who checks her out? I have no claim on her, I remind myself. That's some weird ego shit happening in my subconscious. Caveman shit.

And then, the caveman inside gets louder when I come closer and realize that Dahlia is wearing my flannel shirt. My chest feels like the mayor missed the dunk tank target and hit me in the solar plexus instead. I like her wearing my shirt. I shouldn't like her wearing my shirt but I do. Her dress wasn't warm enough for this weather anyway. Something inside me is pleased she's wearing it. Maybe when I get it back, the shirt will be covered with that apple pie scent of hers.

The twitching of my cock also cannot be ignored. Physically, chemically, primally—I'm still way into her.

I watch her for a minute longer, people milling around me. When one group wanders away from her table, leaving her completely alone for a second, she grabs up the front of my flannel shirt and lifts it to her nose. Her eyes flutter closed.

The arousal I'd felt a minute ago amps up by one thousand percent as I watch. I want to hug her, and then my body wants to fuck her while she's wearing my clothes.

Shit, where did that come from?

I begin to back off. I don't want to be around her while I have this mile-high boner. But then she spots me and waves me over.

"Blake! Hi!" Slightly embarrassed at being caught wearing my flannel, she blushes and takes it off.

"No, you don't have to," I start, rushing toward her.

She flicks a dismissive hand at me. "Don't be silly. I was holding it for you. It just became easier to put it on than set it down and lose it."

The bros wander over to her table from the ring toss game, their girlfriends one step behind them. One of the girls makes a spooky noise as she holds up the brochure about the ghost tour. The other girl seems on board with the idea but their boyfriends are not in to it.

I see Dahlia's inimitable cheerfulness falter a little. Maybe for half a second. I don't like it.

Before I think about what I'm saying, I address the guys. "Listen, that ghost tour is fucking amazing and you need to sign up. Now."

One of the dudes looks at me with an expression that makes me think I might have made him pee his pants. The other one shrugs and grudgingly signs everyone's names on the sheet and pays the fee.

"Wise decision," I say as the men slink away from me and the girls chatter excitedly after thanking me for the recommendation.

Dahlia looks up at me with so much sweetness in her face and a hand to her chest like she's about to make some big declaration of gratitude.

"Save it," I say. I don't need gratitude, because it was only pure machismo that made me feel like coercing those guys into making her happy.

I take my shirt from her, water still dripping from my hair down my neck. "You could have just put it in your bag."

She averts her gaze to her lap. Shyness is not a look I'm used to seeing on her. It's kind of adorable. "I could have, but then your shirt would smell like my breath mints. And then the likelihood of a random emergency tampon flying out of it when I return the shirt to you would be about 3 to 1."

I laugh, and she seems relieved. "Most men don't like tampon jokes."

I shrug. "Most other men are nitwits."

Why did I feel the need to say that? Why does being around her make me want to put all other men in their place? Maybe I should start with, why does it feel so nice to be around her?

I was so hopping mad when I finished at the dunk tank that I was going to march straight over here to tell her she could forget the whole scavenger hunt stop at the bar. But I don't have it in me to say any of that. Instead I'm taken over by the strange sensation that I just want to make her happy. To do anything to keep her smiling.

"You hungry?" I find myself asking.

"Kind of," she says with a grin.

"You wanna ... (gulp) ...grab dinner?"

She sighs regretfully. "I would, but I have to judge the pumpkin pound cake competition in a little while and I want to have a clean palate."

Confused, I tell her that's what I thought the ballot boxes were for.

She brightens up again. She loves explaining how the games work. It's so fucking cute. "Yes, that's for people's choice. To cast a ballot you pay a dollar. But then we have judge's choice, which will decide the grand prize winner."

I shake my head even as my body shivers from wearing wet clothes in the cool air. "Isn't there anyone else?"

She bites her lip. "Well, Amanda Hall has been helping collect the entrance fees from all the vendors and overseeing the ticket booth, otherwise I know she would help."

I sigh. "You need to learn how to delegate."

Her eyes widen. "That's a great idea."

"Oh shit," I say. "No."

"Yes! You judge it with me!"

"I'm wet."

"So go home and dry off and when you get back, we'll do the judging. Deal?"

"No."

"But you're wet and hungry and those pound cakes smell delicious."

True. And so does she.

Her pleading eyes are too much for me.

I grunt out, "Fine," and slosh away to my truck.

Chapter Four

Dahlia

Seven pumpkin pound cakes sit before me on the gingham-covered table. I have so many feelings I don't want to identify or name or cope with, I think I could eat every single one of these deep amber, fragrant desserts all by myself.

I find that thought especially interesting, since, in the two weeks right after Blake and I broke up, I barely ate a thing. As I was a third year transfer at college in my late twenties, living alone in an off campus apartment, I didn't have a core group of friends looking out for me, so I was left alone to wallow. Life as an older student can be very solitary. When I got myself together, I dumped all my feelings and energy into my studies.

And now, after earning my hospitality and history degree, I'm back in my hometown, flirting with disaster all over again. I both dread and anticipate Blake coming back to help me judge the baking competition. Some of me wants to kick myself for putting myself through this, but most of me is elated that he's promised to come back to help me.

Does he actually want to spend time with me or did I just wear him down? Or worse—did he taking pity on me? It has to be obvious how few volunteers I have for this shindig. It's odd. City Hall is in the midst of a mass exodus of employees, which I don't understand. I was beyond thankful for this generous job offer right out of college, but I came in with the understanding that the previous tourism director had up and quit for no apparent reason. Something weird is going on; I just know it.

I'm reminded of my lack of volunteers when Amanda Hall walks up to where I'm sitting. I smile and greet the mayor's wife, but she doesn't seem all that interested in pleasantries.

"I noticed you decided to do a ghost tour tonight," she says, friendly enough at first. But just enough.

"Uhm, yes. Yes, I did. I just decided to do it this morning, to give us a little something edgy to end the festival. It's going to be at Milton House, with a few stops along the way. You remember Esther."

Amanda's face changes from the painted-on smile of a middle-aged politician's wife to something else entirely. "Yes, I do remember Esther. Poor dear. That's so thoughtful of you to want to include that drafty old house in the festival. You're so brave. It's probably a good thing you don't know the real story of that house, or you might cancel the whole thing."

I smile at her. "Oh, I do. I went through all the archives and news articles dating back to the time the house was built. I know all about it."

She eyes me for what feels like the world's longest minute. "I see. Well, then I guess I was mistaken. You've clearly got it all figured out. Good luck to you, sweetie."

Amanda smiles sweetly at me, but that smile doesn't reach

her eyes and it's got a whole story behind it. She walks away and I have to fight off a full-body shiver.

"You look like you've seen a ghost."

I jump at the man's voice, but for an entirely different reason. It's relief, even though Blake means it as a corny joke.

"Very funny," I say with a smirk.

He chuckles but plops down next to me with a serious expression. "No, I'm serious. You look spooked. What happened?"

The look on his face is all seriousness and concern. I feel a familiar warmth flood through me. *Don't get attached to that look, Dahlia Jane. Don't you dare get attached.*

"I'm fine," I say with my usual bright smile. "I'm all good."

I can tell right away he doesn't believe that for a second. "Out with it. What happened?"

I fidget with the serving knife while replaying for him the whole scene with the mayor's wife. When I'm done, Blake looks wary.

"I do not like the sound of that," he says. "Wonder what she meant?"

I shrug. "I don't know. I'm not going to worry about it right now. Come on, let's eat some pound cake! I'm starving."

Blake studies my face, making me blush. "Yeah," he says, his voice sounding oddly rough as he stares at me. "I could definitely eat something."

Oh god. *He didn't mean anything else by that. Right?*

Feeling his eyes on me as I slice off a piece of cake for him, my hands shake slightly. Not even the most objective, logical part of my brain can deny it now. He totally meant that as innuendo. He wanted to make me remember things— things even more delicious than cake. And there's really only one thing more delicious than cake, and it's not pumpkin pie.

Oh god.

I hand him his plate, but he doesn't take it from me.

Without breaking eye contact, like he's daring me to look away, he grabs up the piece of cake with his hands and shoves it into his mouth. He chews it up with the most inappropriate yum-yum noises I've ever heard, and then, as if that weren't enough, licks his fingers clean. Slowly. All the while daring me to look away from him.

If his goal is to make my nipples tighten and make me feel lightheaded? Mission accomplished.

Chapter Five

Blake

Dahlia knows I'm flirting now. Likes it. Wants me to keep doing it, unless I'm painfully mistaken.

And as much of a pain in the ass as this whole festival can be, I might be having a fun time. When the little 12-year-old girl who wins the cake contest hoists the grand prize antique Bundt pan over her head and hollers like she's just won the Women's World Cup, it's a nice moment. I'm not made of stone. I consider the possibility that maybe *I'm* the one who's the actual pain in the ass.

Dahlia stares at me incredulously as I stay around to help her shake out the gingham tablecloths and pack up the tables from the contest. "You can go if you want," she says. "It's almost time for trick or treating. You probably have things to do at the bar."

I kick at a particularly stubborn collapsible leg of the banquet table and it folds with a loud clank. "What kind of a man would I be if I left you to do all the clean up? Kenny can handle things while I'm gone."

The way she looks at me with that shy, slightly embarrassed smile is so endearing that I want to grab her and kiss her so hard she forgets her long list of responsibilities for the entire evening.

Once we finish cleaning up, she walks with me toward the bar.

"You've done a lot of work, do you know that?"

Dahlia waves me off. "I've had some help."

"For as long as I can remember the Fall Festival has consisted of one face painter and an apple bobbing contest that caused an outbreak of the flu. So yes, you are amazing and I'm incredibly proud of you."

She makes a dismissive snort but in the golden twilight I can see her grinning.

"I mean it. Did you see the look on that girl's face when you handed her that stupid bundt pan? You're a rock star."

Dahlia laughs. "You'd better stop or I'm going to get a very big head."

She stops walking and turns to me. The fading gold and purple sunset makes her skin glow even more than usual, and her eyes sparkle. I think I see a tear there, and I'm kicking myself for going too far with my compliments. We stare at each other, both of us remembering the way we used to be together. I remember it every day. I have to stop kidding myself; I never stopped thinking about her.

"Thank you for helping me today," she says.

I chew on the inside of my cheek. The thing I want to do has the potential to go really well or really fuck everything up again for the both of us.

I don't know how long we stand there, making eyes at each other.

With a regretful sigh, she points out that trick or treating is starting soon and that I need to head back to the bar to get ready."

I mutter, "Yeah, you're right."

"And then there's the scavenger hunt, plus the bar is open late tonight. You have a long night ahead of you," she says.

I nod. "Yup. And you should go get some rest before your first annual ghost tour."

She sighs. "Yes. I really should."

I give her a wink. "Get going. And I'll see you tonight for our big Halloween bet."

Dahlia exhales and treats me with a small smile. "Right. Tour starts at midnight at the picnic shelters, and then I'll meet you at the haunted house."

Chapter Six

Dahlia

After leaving Blake at the bar, I float off toward the square to hand out candy to a couple hundred little fairies, zombies, firefighters, Captain Americas and ghosts. After the trick or treating chaos wraps up, I head home for a quick nap. I snuggle down under my comforter and set my alarm. But before I set it, I quickly check social media to see the progress of the scavenger hunt.

To my surprise, I see that Blake has already been tagged in about a dozen pictures by participants in the game. And he doesn't look all that upset about it. The Blake I know hates all of this nonsense. It becomes abundantly clear that he's doing this for me. All of it.

A part of me feels bad for manipulating him into helping out so much today. But I realize why I've sought him out. Because for me, it's always been Blake. He was my first everything. My first kiss, my first sex partner, my first love. My first and only.

I go to sleep for a couple of hours with one question on my mind: Is he playing along just to get me back in his arms, or has he actually changed for the better?

Chapter Seven

Blake

I MOSEY OVER TO THE ROTTING PICNIC SHELTER WHERE THE ghost tour is scheduled to begin and end.

As I wait for Dahlia, I look over the neglected structure and think about how I'd love to have the chance to fix it up.

I recently put in a bid to the city council to let me take on the project. I could do it myself almost entirely in my Gramps's wood shop. And since I'm not a large construction company and have no employees, I know my bid has to be lower than anyone else's.

I don't understand a lot about local politics but I know I saw something in the paper about the council getting into a huge argument with the finance department over the project, and the whole thing getting tabled until the next meeting. Which kind of sucks, as it would have been nice to have new shelters built in time for visitors to use on the day of the festival. Then, in the following week's newspaper, I recall reading about the finance director quitting. The past couple of years has seen several department heads quit unexpectedly, which is how the city came to offer the tourism job to Dahlia.

City government and finance might not make any sense to me, but hell, I'd probably rehab every picnic shelter in the entire town for free if Dahlia asked me to. Surely that's a bid not even our mayor could refuse.

While I wait for the tour to start, I reach into my back pocket and count out my tips again. Dahlia was right. The bar ended up making a huge profit off the scavenger hunt, and the clientele wasn't nearly as obnoxious as I'd first assumed they would be.

I would normally stay extra late on Halloween, but I have new plans, which, if all goes well, will take up the rest of my night, so I called in a couple of extra servers to help Kenny. I'd rather spend time with Dahlia than squeeze out more tips for me from drunk customers after midnight.

Chapter Eight

Dahlia

IT'S MIDNIGHT, THE TOUR IS READY TO BEGIN, AND AT first, it looks like I have no participants.

It makes no sense. The entire town came out for the festival today, which means the ten sign ups I had originally was already a fairly modest start.

But now, nobody has even bothered to show up, not the people who signed up at the festival, nor those who registered on the city website. In fact, now that I'm looking at my phone, the sign-up page that I'd added to the city website has been erased. Why would people sign up, pay the fee, and then not come?

I slump down at one of the picnic tables and allow myself to feel sad for five minutes, in the dark, with nobody looking.

"This where the tour starts?"

I look up, and Blake is standing over me, looking confused.

Quickly, I wipe away a tear that I stupidly let fall. "It's cancelled. Nobody showed up."

"Listen, I paid my $20 online and I expect a tour."

Now I'm the one who is confused. "It was a dollar, for charity."

"Oh," he says with a mischievous wink. "Well, I guess I overpaid then."

I need to set the record straight. "Blake, I know you only signed up because you felt sorry for me."

He crosses his arms over his wide chest. "First of all, I didn't sign up out of pity. I signed up because I wanted to ... to support you. Do you understand the difference?"

I bite my lip to keep the grin from spreading, but who am I kidding. I can't hide my smile any more than I can stop the warm fuzzies that spread through me any time Blake shows me his tender side.

"Well? Who are we waiting around for? Lead on, tour guide. I want my money's worth."

Chapter Nine

Blake

I HOIST MY BACKPACK AND SLEEPING BAG, AND GRAB Dahlia's things from her.

"I can carry those," she says.

I ignore her protest and press her to get on with the tour.

The first stop on the tour is, of course, the graveyard.

It should come as no surprise to me that Dahlia has done her homework. I learn a few things about the town's founders, about some local war heroes, murders, historic battles, stagecoach robbery gangs, famous criminals, and unfortunate disease outbreaks. I don't say it out loud because I don't want her getting her hopes up that she's got a chance of winning this ridiculous bet we made, but this tour is not bananas at all. I think a lot of people would find it really interesting.

When I see Dahlia shivering, I ask her to skip over the vacant lot where everyone thinks there used to be a hotel where Lincoln once slept.

"But..." she begins to argue, but I'm overcome with the urge to warm her up with a huge bear hug.

I can't hold back. My arms pull her in close, unzipping my coat and wrapping it around her. Her slim-fitting trench coat might look hot as hell on her, but there's no way it's keeping her warm enough.

That's my job now.

The more time I spend with her, the more I feel as though we have things to talk about. Dahlia's body stiffens at first, not expecting my embrace. I wait for her to push me away or scold me. She would be right to. But instead, she relaxes against my chest and gingerly squeezes me back, her arms around my ribcage.

"Let's get to the main event now, D."

She steps back, her eyes wide.

"I don't mean it that way," I say. "I mean let's get to the Milton House and out of the cold so we can talk. I think you and I have a few things to hash out before the night is over, don't you?"

Chapter Ten

Dahlia

So, I think, as I smirk to myself while unlocking the front door of Milton House. He also wants to talk about "things." Things that happened in the past? Things that I sense are happening between us now? I can't tell for sure.

Don't get too excited, Dahlia. He might just want talk about "keeping things casual and seeing where they go."

Just like the day before I transferred out of state.

When I twist the key in the lock, the heavy oak door creaks open and we step inside.

I switch on the lantern to guide our way, and it illuminates the front room with a soft white glow. Something feels off inside the house, like somebody has been here. It makes no sense, though, as I'm the only one with a key and I changed the locks as soon as the tourism bureau took possession of the house. I examine the door for any signs of forced entry but there are none.

And then I realize it's not the presence of someone, but

the opposite, as if someone is missing and the house is unsettled. I don't really believe anything specific about the afterlife, but something weird is going on here.

"What's wrong?" Blake asks, stepping close to me.

"I don't know. Probably just Halloween excitement playing tricks on me."

Blake towers over me. "If you want to get out of here, just say the word."

I narrow my eyes at him. "What, you think I'm scared already?"

"No, you just looked a little spaced out for a minute there. If you're tired..."

I stand up on my toes for emphasis but my eyes can only manage to be level with his Adam's apple. "I'm not tired. I'm not scared. But I am curious what things you wanted to talk about."

He blinks down at me for a moment then shakes his head. "Listen. I know you did a lot of preparation for this ghost tour, so let's have it. I want to hear everything."

I try to be the cool, low maintenance chick. "It's fine," I say. "We don't have to...I mean, I know you think this ghost stuff is baloney, so we can just skip it if you want."

"D, give me the story. And then we'll talk." He sees right through me. And I like it.

I switch off the lantern, then pull out my flashlight and shine it up my face from under my chin. "But be prepared to have the bejeezus scared out of you."

He chuckles. "You know you're the only person on earth who still looks cute when you do that dorky flashlight thing on your face?"

He's trying to charm me. And it's working. Before I let him distract me any further, I start my speech and lead him through the front parlor, putting my flashlight away and relighting the lantern.

"There's no electricity; it was shut off shortly after Esther passed. I decided to wait to turn it back on until I can have everything inspected. So watch your step, please." I switch to my tour guide voice. "The Milton House was built by Captain James Milton in 1899 and was passed down through the generations." I continue on with the entire history of the house, leading Blake through the front hall, the parlor, and dining room, making note of all the changes and minor upgrades, fun trivia and the Milton family history.

In the dark, I can feel Blake's eyes on me. The thought of it makes me feel a little shaky. I put out a hand on the wall to steady my tired ankles when I hear something crash to the floor.

I gasp and shine my light toward the sound of tinkling glass. Bending over to get a closer look, I see it's a picture of the late John Milton, Esther's husband, that had been on a shelf nearby.

"That's so odd," I say, picking it up, careful not to cut myself.

"You totally knocked that off with your hand, D."

"No, I swear I did not," I breathe.

Blake scoffs. We make our way to the kitchen while I continue with the tour. "It was back here in the kitchen where Esther Milton first reported unusual activity in the house. She had come downstairs for a midnight snack and, according to her police report, a figure was standing outside the window, perfectly still, watching her. Police responded, but they found nothing. When it happened again a few weeks later and the police again found nothing, she called the newspaper to come and investigate. According to the newspaper archives I've read through, the reporters also found nothing amiss. At that point, she decided it was the ghost of her late husband, and she started calling psychics, ghost hunters, and just about anybody else who would listen to her.

"Soon afterward, she began to report more and more mysterious incidents at the house..."

We're headed up the stairs to the bedrooms as I list off all the evidence of haunting. "Flickering lights," I say.

"Probably just old wiring," Blake mutters.

"...Kitchen drawers found open that weren't left open..."

"Forgetfulness."

"Sounds of footsteps on the stairs when she was alone..."

Blake grunts behind me. "Foundation settling."

I shake my head but I can't help but smile; I can't tell if he's trying to convince me or convince himself.

Chapter Eleven

BLAKE

I KEEP UP WITH HER RUNNING COMMENTARY THROUGHOUT the tour. I don't believe any of it to be true, but I have to admit, Dahlia is pretty convincing. Was there ever any doubt she would be?

I stay close behind her, considering whether I want to choose the perfect moment to make her jump. Would she throttle me? Probably.

Maybe I could pretend I see a ghost, just for a laugh.

None of it seems right though. She's having too much fun, and she barely pauses to breathe while she's throwing so much information at me.

"...and then as Esther's health deteriorated, the sightings increased in frequency. She saw people at the windows at night..."

"Tricks of the light."

"...strange objects left on her porch..."

"Neighborhood kids playing tricks on her."

"...and odd sounds coming from the basement..."

"Foundation quirks. Squirrels. Mice. Birds stuck in the chimneys. Water leaks."

Dahlia has no idea how beautiful she is in the lantern light as she guides me through the master bedroom and the guest bedrooms. She's switched her topic from the home's history to talking about her plans to restore the house to its original look, down to antique furnishings in all the rooms.

We stop at one of the guest rooms. Some branches of tall tree, wild looking in the moonlight, butt up against the window on the far wall. Leaning against the opposite wall is a huge ornate mirror that was never hung on the wall.

"Some people might agree with you that all the phenomena has a rational explanation. And there was a time where Mrs. Milton herself might have dismissed all these things. But after several years of incidents, she had gained a bit of notoriety and wanted to turn her house into a bed and breakfast. You know, to use the haunting to create a source of income. But the town council at the time refused to change the zoning to help her out. It's sad, but she never got to see her dream materialize," Dahlia says.

"Because she turned out to be completely nuts?"

"She wasn't nuts, it was just nobody believed in her, and soon she stopped believing in herself. When I moved back here, I became interested in local history and I visited with her frequently. She really was a wealth of knowledge. I'm glad I got to know her as a person, too. She was so kind, and always had cookies waiting for me whenever I'd come to visit. By that time, she got a full-time nurse in the house and the unexplained phenomena quieted down. Some people said it was because the nurse got her medications straightened out. Or maybe the ghosts finally decided to leave her alone."

"Is that why she gave the house to the tourism department? Because you went to visit her?"

Dahlia shrugs like it was not a big deal. "She was a lot of fun to talk to. It made me sad that I hadn't gotten to know her sooner. If I hadn't transferred away, maybe I could have helped her write a book about her memories. Who knows what could have happened if I'd stayed?"

Her question hangs in the air between us. She turns and looks up at me.

"Do you … have any other regrets?" I ask.

"I regret not being here for Gramps's funeral. I regret not being there for you."

I open my mouth to reply when she nearly jumps out of her skin and latches on to my arm.

"Oh my god! Did you see that?"

My heart thuds in my chest and I instinctively slide my arm around her. "What? Where?"

"Something moved, just beyond the light, at the end of the hallway!"

"Stop," I say.

"I'm serious, Blake."

She is serious; I can feel her trembling.

"Probably just a mouse, but let's go check it out if it will make you feel better?"

Who knew she could be so jumpy on a tour that she orchestrated? Or maybe she's acting. If that's the case, hand her the Oscar, please.

I take the lantern out of her hand and lead the way, my arm fixed around her. We creep toward the end of the hall, and I keep the light trained on the master bedroom door.

We both startle when we see the rocking chair by the window move on its own.

"What the fuck!" I yell.

Dahlia grips me around the waist and yelps just seconds before we see a small, shadowy ball of fur dart out the open window.

"What was that?" she whispers.

"That was a squirrel. But the bigger question is, why is that window open? Did you leave it open?"

"No!" she says.

I go into the room to close the window, Dahlia melded to me.

"That's just the kind of thing Mrs. Milton told me about. She said back in the day, she used to find random windows open.

"She probably forgot," I reply, carefully shutting the window and closing the curtain. "You'd be surprised how easily we forget we leave windows, doors, drawers, cabinets open. In any case, that was a tree-climbing rodent and not a ghost. A ghost wouldn't open a window anyway; they can walk through walls, can't they?"

"Oh, sweet Blake," she sighs, sounding like I should know better. "If they don't know they're a ghost, they may try to open doors and windows."

"Except that they're not real," I remind her.

She looks at me like I've just kicked her dog. "That poor woman spent years telling everyone she knew that she was being visited by the ghost of her dead husband and nobody believed her. Who are we to say she was wrong?"

I wrap my arms around her and pull her close, her shoulders drooping.

"May I tell you what I think? I think you've gotten too invested in this ghost thing and you don't want to let her memory down."

"That's ridiculous."

"Is it?"

"You're just trying to convince me. That's not the same as proving ghosts don't exist."

I sigh and pull my phone out of my pocket. "Listen. It's

one a.m. and I think we're both tired. Let's go home and we'll call it a draw."

"No. I'm not leaving," she says.

"Well, I'm not leaving you here, scared and alone in the dark."

"I'm not scared."

"I don't know why."

"Because he's a friendly ghost."

"Why would a friendly ghost do things like leave windows open and freak out his own wife with footsteps on the staircase?"

"Because he wanted his wife to feel like she wasn't alone. And, maybe, when we die, our attempts to comfort the living don't translate. Maybe some of our messages come through damaged. And that's why it's unsettling. Maybe her husband was just trying to say he loved her, but showed up as a creaking staircase. Just like when the living try to communicate, it doesn't always go so well."

The subtext is so obvious it punches me in the gut. Two years ago, she told me she loved me, and I freaked. Jesus. What the hell is wrong with me?

I swallow hard. "Dahlia..."

"Settle down, big guy. We haven't finished the tour. We still have the most haunted part of the house to explore. The basement."

"D, come on. Let's skip it."

Her eyes pop wide at me and she stands on tip toe. "You're a big chicken!"

I huff. "No, I am not."

"If we don't go down to the basement, then you forfeit the bet and I win."

I scrape my fingers through my hair and mutter, "This is ridiculous."

"Well, then, you lose, is all I'm saying."

"All right, fine."

Dahlia opens the door under the staircase and begins her descent, me still holding the lantern. I put out a hand to stop her.

"I can't let you go down there first."

"What do you think is going to happen? Wow, you really are scared, aren't you?"

"No, but what if there are snakes or spiders or bugs or who knows what else? What kind of a person would I be if you got a snake bite before I did?"

"OK, fine, I'll let you hold on to your chivalry for now."

"I appreciate that."

Shining the lantern and her flashlight ahead of us, we make our way down the stairs.

The dark, dank, cool space feels even more like death and doom than the rest of the house. I don't understand why, but something in the air makes my blood pressure rise and the hairs on the back of my neck tingle.

We shine our lights around to get a better look. It's not what I was expecting. The space is divided into rooms like someone had begun to build an apartment down here. There are studs, but no actual walls.

"Esther Milton reported noises in the basement at least once a month to police during the height of the apparent haunting. At first they came to investigate but they never found anything. After a while, they stopped taking her seriously and then she simply stopped calling them. She told me she decided it was just the ghost of her husband looking after her."

"Looking after her by making weird noises in a creepy basement? Might want to find a better service provider from the afterlife, dude, 'cause you really got shit wrong."

"Talking to a ghost now? That's belief. You lose."

"Nice try, Dahlia Jane."

She laughs. "The last time you called me that…oh my god."

She doesn't respond but her eyes widen and I feel her full-body shiver next to me.

"What is it?"

"Did you feel that cold spot?"

"It's a basement; it's probably coming from the vents."

"No," she says. "It's not the same as a draft."

My nerves waver a little, though my mind tries to keep a hold on the most logical explanation. I study her face in the lantern light. If she's acting, she's definitely fooling me. "I feel it on my skin, even inside my coat. Under my skin."

"This isn't funny, D."

We examine all the partitions for the source of the breeze but don't find it.

What we do find, however, in the farthest corner of the basement is one small room, is an old wooden chair overturned, and above it, a rope hanging from a support beam in the shape of a noose. The rope is swinging ever so slightly, like it's being pushed—or swayed—by a draft.

The image of this completely sucks all the air out of my lungs. Dahlia whimpers and I try to pull her back but she doesn't move.

"This is it," she says. "This is what Esther and John want us to see."

I suddenly get the distinct impression she's winding me up.

"So help me, D, if you're pranking me right now."

She shakes her head. "No. No, this is the room where her husband used to go. Esther told me he used to come down here to think and to mess around with his old train sets. She was never allowed down here."

"D, I don't like this. Let's get out of here."

She shakes her head. "No. She told me there was something down here, there was something down here he didn't want her to see."

An ice-cold wind rushes past my ears, blocking out all noise around me, and next thing I know the door at the top of the stairs has slammed shut.

Dahlia screams.

"Whoa!" I shout.

I throw one arm around Dahlia and pull her up the stairs with me. She trembles like a leaf in my arm. "It's OK, baby. I'm getting you out of here."

She's not speaking, not making any noise at all, other than her teeth chattering uncontrollably like she's standing in a meat locker. She's either truly freezing, or frightened out of her mind.

Chapter Twelve

Dahlia

I HAVE NO IDEA WHAT'S GOING ON, ONLY THAT I CAN'T control the bone-deep cold pressing against my chest as Blake carries me up the stairs.

He kicks open the door to the hall, but I don't even hear the doorjamb splinter. All I hear are my teeth chattering and a wind like a blizzard rushing around my ears. But why isn't my hair moving if I feel like I'm in the middle of a windstorm at the North Pole?

"Change of plans. We're getting out of here," he says when he reaches the hallway.

He has me halfway to the front door when I try to pull away.

"Stop, D, I'm going to drop you."

"P-put me down."

"No," he says, charging the door.

With all my might, I struggle against his grip.

Gruffly he gives in and sets me down gently on my feet. His hands never leave my hips while he questions me.

"All right, I put you down but now you gotta tell me what's going on."

I shake my head. "We're close."

He nods. "Yeah, close to you completely losing your mind because somebody is playing tricks on you. Let's go. This sleepover is cancelled."

I shake my head more emphatically, but it only causes my whole body to erupt in a fresh bout of intense trembling. My breathing is shallow, and a feeling of dread seems to be pouring out of the walls the closer we get to the door to leave.

"She doesn't want me to leave. I can't leave," I plead with him.

"I'm putting my foot down. This is enough, D."

I grab his shirt. "It's n-not about the bet anymore. S-something really bad happened here. The c-closer we get to leaving the house, the more it feels like...like I might d-die, Blake. P-please."

He wraps his arms around me, pinning my arms to my sides to still my tremors. "You're having a panic attack. Come on, let's go to the kitchen door and try to go out that way. One step at a time."

He holds my hand and guides me to the kitchen. But as soon as we're within a few feet of the kitchen door, same thing. The trembling spikes, my guts feel like I'm riding a plummeting elevator, and my air passageways feel half blocked.

"I'm so cold, I can't stop shaking," I squeak through my constricted throat. "And I can barely breathe."

Blake tries to still me by putting his big arms around me, telling me to breathe in slowly with him.

"This is not a p-panic attack. This house is h-h-haunted," I whimper.

Blake runs one hand through his hair and mutters. "Fuck. Come here, D."

He scoops me up and carries me up the staircase. "Wh-where...?" I start to say, but he has no more patience for me and my full-body shakes.

"As far away from the basement as possible without leaving," he says.

Inside the guest room, Blake sets me down on the end of the bed. I watch curiously as he unzips my sleeping bag to make a blanket on the bare mattress.

He begins to undress me and my panic rises in my throat. But, I remind myself, this is Blake. He wouldn't... "Blake, w-what...?"

"I don't know if this is what I'm supposed to do for...whatever the hell is going on with you...but this is what we're doing."

I acquiesce but only because I trust him completely. He would never purposefully do anything to hurt me.

He tosses my trench coat to the floor and helps me slip out of my boots and my dress. Now only in my underwear, he helps me lie face down on the bed.

I'm still trembling, but not as intensely as I was downstairs. I turn my head on the sleeping bag to look at his reflection in the window. Everything looks wild and eerie in the lantern glow. I watch him take off his jacket and shirt and undress himself down to his boxer briefs. It's then I realize what he's doing—he's taking care of me the way he used to do when we were dating. The idea of it nudges my heart. The memory of it would make me full-out cry but I'm so scared and cold and freaked out, no other emotions can take hold.

Whenever I'd get so stressed and overwhelmed about my grades or work myself up into a ball of nerves over my term papers to the point of not sleeping or eating, Blake would convince me to take a break and lie down on my bed for non-sexual "skin on skin time."

"B-Blake, this isn't term paper stress. This is s-something else."

But in the next second he's hovering over me, his palms running the lengths of my arms and legs, gradually pressing his weight down on top of my back.

"Let me know when it's too much and I'll back off," he whispers in my ear, brushing my hair away from my neck.

"You must be freezing," I say as the trembling beginning to subside.

"Kinda," he says. Blake grudgingly gets off me for a second to grab his flannel-lined sleeping bag. He unzips it and covers the both of us with it. My skin misses him in the few seconds it takes for him to do this, and I realize my heart is at risk of getting attached to him again.

Trapped body heat combined with skin on skin contact is actually working. His big chest blankets me and I can feel his chest muscles ripple against my shoulder blades while he warms my arms. The smell from the flannel lining of his sleeping bag hits me. Oh boy, do I remember what we used to do in the woods inside this exact sleeping bag. He adds a little more of his weight and I sigh.

"Am I too heavy? Just say so."

I close my eyes. His stubble warms my cheek.

"Too heavy? God no. Don't hold back."

"If you're sure," he says. Blake's voice vibrates all through me; it's the sweetest feeling in the whole world. Oh yeah, I'm definitely in danger of getting hurt all over again. But I'm under this crazy spell of not just attraction but of affection. His need to take care of me was one of the most endearing things about him, back when we were together.

I feel a connection with him on every inch of my exposed

skin. Even his toes are linked up with mine. Something about it not only calms me down but squeezes my heart. It's so heavy and comforting and loving, it's making even more happy memories of our time together two years ago come flooding back.

Blake's covered dick is wedged between my ass cheeks in the most innocent way possible, as much as it can be while I'm wearing cheeky undies. There seems to be no sexual end goal to what he's doing; it's just comfort. He knows how to block out the world for me. He silences all my racing thoughts.

The trembling has finally stopped. My breathing normalizes. My skin warms. The hideous feeling of dread in my guts evaporates. I find myself on the verge of plummeting into blissful sleep.

My voice cracks as I whisper, "Thank you."

Chapter Thirteen

Her emotional "thank you" pushes away all the remaining stubbornness from of my chest.

Why did I ever let her get away? Why did I push her so hard to let me go when she went away to finish college? She loved me and I convinced myself that breaking up was for her own good. When she told me she loved me, it was so pure and sweet and raw, but it caught me off guard. In my head I'm kicking myself.

Time to lay it all out on the line and see where it lands.

"I should have asked you to stay," I whisper into her neck.

"Blake, I know why you did it."

"Let me finish. I should have told you when Gramps died. I knew you would forgive me for everything and come home immediately to be with me, to help me. But I foolishly didn't want you to forgive me for that reason. I felt I didn't deserve for you to help me through my grief. I thought I deserved to be alone. You told me you loved me and I ended it. I thought

I would hold you back if we tried making our relationship work long distance, so I broke things off with you.

"I'm sorry; I shouldn't have done that. Sorry isn't even the right word. I'm disgusted with what I did. I beat myself up over it every day. And when you came home six months ago and walked into my bar, I thought the universe was punishing me. I felt I didn't deserve you, but I deserved the torture of seeing you every day. I should have handled a lot of things very differently and I regret...everything."

I brush my hand along the soft strands of auburn hair splayed out against the sleeping bag, and it's there that I feel dampness.

"D? Are you OK?"

I feel her nod and I hear her sniffle. "I'm sorry too," she says.

I try to shush her but she needs to talk just as much as I do.

Chapter Fourteen

Dahlia

Blake's words, his strong body blanketed over me, and his warm breath on my neck make me feel so safe that I let everything I've been holding on to ever since I moved back home spill out.

"I shouldn't have been so angry. I should have believed you when you said you thought it was for the best that we broke up," I say. "I thought you were scared of commitment and I called you a coward. That wasn't true."

He breathes a small laugh against my skin. "You called me a lot more than that. Things I'd never heard come out of those perfect lips of yours."

On the street at noon on a Sunday, just as people were leaving church, as I recall. I squeeze my eyes shut at the uncomfortable memory. "And I'm sorry that I scared you away when I said I loved you. I should have waited for you to say it first."

The sudden roughness in his voice almost scares me.

"Stop it. Don't ever apologize for loving someone. Be proud you had the guts to say it. I wish I had."

There he goes, squeezing my heart and making it impossible for me not to fall for him again. His fingers roaming through my hair send pleasing tingles through my body.

"Let's never do that again," he says.

I laugh softly. "You mean never again have a fight on a public street and call each other names and hurt each other and then stop speaking? Yeah, I promise to hold up my end of that deal."

Blake exhales a sexy sigh and gently hoists himself off me, while keeping his arms and knees on the mattress, caging me in. My body immediately misses the pressure of him. "No. I mean let's never break up again."

He waits patiently for the words to land in my brain. When they do, I flip myself over on the bed to face him. I open my mouth to speak but the words won't come out. I fit my hands along his stubbled jawline. His wide, questioning grin seems to light up the space around us.

"I love you, D. I never stopped loving you."

With those words, he's just wrung out the last drop of my resolve to protect myself. For maybe the first time in my life I'm at a complete loss for words. So it's a good thing no more words are necessary for kissing.

Blake's lips ease against mine in a familiar slide that's so tender and full of promise I couldn't resist even if I had a good reason to. I slip my fingers around to the back of his neck and pull him closer. My lips know his lips and his know mine. They've missed each other. I know he's thinking the same thing as his suction intensifies and his tongue tastes my lips, first the bottom then the top. Our tongues tease each other until our mutual need to claim the other takes over.

Hands gripping each other's hair, tongues tangling, teeth scraping, legs entwining. This moment feels like we've just unlocked the door to a once-sad, empty room full of memories and thrown open the curtains to let the light flood in.

I can't control the moans that tumble from my mouth into his.

Blake pauses to breathe against my neck. "Never again," he mutters. "Never letting you slip away again." His pause to breathe is familiar, too. He's restraining himself; I can feel him fighting back against his instinct to take me hard and fast.

He growls when I rake my nails over his chest. His mouth paints kisses down my neck to the valley between my breasts. I weave my fingers into his golden locks and pull him closer to urge him on. He gently scrapes his teeth over one of my hard nipples, then the other, before sucking each of them through the material of my bra, ramping up my excitement.

"Tell me what you want, Dahlia." I let go of his hair and slide my hand down his chest and lower, following the deep V-lines of his lower abdomen until his hard length presses into my palm.

An unintelligible noise of pleasure erupts from the back of his throat. The tip has already breached his waistband, so I help it along by tugging his underwear down his thighs.

He grunts in relief when his cock springs free. I feel it twitch in my hand as I pet it. "D, it's been so long I might not last if you keep rubbing me like that. I want a taste of what I've been missing first."

I gasp when I gather his meaning. His mouth covers mine hungrily once more before flicking open the clasp of my bra. His warm mouth worships my breasts, suckling each of my tight peaks until I'm nearly mad with need. My thighs clamp around him, and my hips grind against his hard cock.

He chuckles softly. "Now I told you to stop rubbing. Guess I'm going to have to get my face between your thighs right this instant."

A giggle bursts out of me when I realize something. "Technically it is November 1, so you have my permission to commence with pie season."

His forehead drops heavily to my stomach as he groans and I laugh harder. "Oh my god, D, you did not."

"I couldn't help myself," I say. One moment I'm trying to control the impulse to crack myself up, the next moment my arousal skyrockets as my big, golden god takes back what belongs to him.

Before I can object—not that I want to—he disappears my undies in under three seconds, and spreads me wide for him. He's done restraining himself. Good.

The sensation of Blake's strong lips at my core, tasting me deeply, forcefully, does not simply make me forget all the stress of the previous day, but might also make me forget my own name. The strange dread that surprised me earlier tonight is ancient history.

He alternates between slow, savoring kisses and teasing licks. Every inch of my pussy is drenched with my arousal and his kisses. By the time he sucks my clit into his mouth, I'm so on fire that a volcanic orgasm destroys me almost instantly.

"Oh god! Blake!" I cry as the waves crash over me. The vibrations of his moans against my sensitive skin draw out the most intense aftershocks I've ever felt in my life. I shiver again, but this time not out of fear.

"I need to kiss you," I whimper.

Blake shares my taste with me, and I confess to him I haven't been with anyone else since we were together last. "I guess I'm out of practice, or I would have lasted longer for you."

He rumbles against my mouth. "I couldn't even look at another woman after you left, because I know no other woman would look at me the way you do."

Chapter Fifteen

BLAKE

"ROLL OVER FOR ME AND WATCH ME IN THE MIRROR. I want you to see what I see."

My instructions are met with a ragged gasp, followed by Dahlia's eager compliance. She flips over so she's face-down on the bed and turns her face toward the mirror to look at us together.

I cage her legs with mine on the mattress and tease the backs of her thighs and her round ass with my hard length. I keep eye contact with her in the mirror.

"There you are. There's my girl. No, don't turn your head; I want you to look at me. Look at me in the mirror while I fuck all the stress out of you."

Both of us look like a sexy, crazy mess. She releases a deep, satisfied sigh as I slip into her sex from behind.

Chapter Sixteen

Dahlia

The sweet, meditative friction of Blake's massive cock makes my entire being feel full.

I never thought my body could feel a need more powerful than the last time he was inside me two years ago, but here I am, writhing under him, my fingers locked onto the sheets and my knuckles turning white as I ascend toward another mind-blowing climax.

I grit my teeth and press my forehead into the mattress while Blake continues his slow rhythm of deep, healing thrusts.

"Look back at me," he rumbles, stippling my shoulder with a line of wet, sloppy kisses.

I do as he says and turn my head to look, but then something catches my eye in the mirror.

I hear the scrape of a branch against the window before my eyes register what I'm seeing. I gasp in fright. I lift my head off the blanket and my eyes dart around frantically.

"Baby, baby, what is it?" He stops his movements, his face trained on me but my gaze is locked on something in the mirror.

Another face in the darkness. It's at the window.

I can't speak. I can't scream. I'm frozen in place and the horrible dread in my stomach is back.

Blake follows the look of terror on my face and he finally sees it too.

"What the fuck!" he roars.

By the time he's stood and located his jeans, the face in the mirror is gone. I hear more sounds of scraping branches against the window, followed by sounds of rustling, twigs snapping and a small thud on the ground.

"Someone or something was in the tree outside the window," I say, my voice shaking as I run to the window and try to make out any shapes below us on the ground. "Please don't go out there, Blake."

But he's out the door before I finish saying the words.

Chapter Seventeen

BLAKE

I SHOULD HAVE KNOWN IT WAS A TRAP.

Almost as soon as I throw open the front door of the house to investigate, they have me.

Who "they" are, I don't know. But there are two of them, one on each arm. Someone shoves something over my face and the smell of burlap fills my nostrils. I fight with everything in me, kicking, thrashing, roaring to make as much noise as I can. For a brief moment, the two thugs lose control of me, and for a millisecond the sack slips off. It's enough time for me to catch a glimpse in the glow of someone's flashlight: a logo on the side of a truck. Mason Construction.

I commit what I see to memory just as something heavy and metal strikes the back of my head. My hands are tied behind me, and I'm vaguely aware that I'm being shoved into a trunk as everything fades to black.

Chapter Eighteen

Dahlia

I SCRAMBLE AROUND TO GATHER MY CLOTHES, ALL THE while hearing terrifying noises outside. I try to keep it together as I throw on my dress, all the while hearing struggling, shouting and the sound of car or truck doors shut before multiple vehicles drive away in a hurry.

I make for the door, lantern in hand, trying to dial 911 with trembling fingers. Someone or something grabs me from behind. I scream but my voice is muffled by a gloved hand covering my mouth. I bite down hard. A woman screams, and for a second I think it's me. But it's coming from whoever it is who grabbed me. The person knocks my legs out from under me, and my phone goes flying as I fall. My assailant pins me to the floor, my hands behind my back. Whoever it is breathing as heavily as I am. Maybe more so. Keeping control of my fear, I infer that my attacker is female, and I think I can take her out if I need to. She's out of breath from her efforts to subdue me.

So, I calm myself, and let whoever it is believe she has the upper hand. She wraps what feels like a length of thick, rough rope around my wrists. My brain somehow recalls a trick I saw somewhere, probably during a late night true crime documentary binge, so I clasp my hands together and hold my elbows wide as she binds my hands. I just hope it works to create enough slack to rescue myself when the opportunity comes.

Chapter Nineteen

BLAKE

I REALIZE I'M STILL IN THE TRUNK OF A CAR WHEN I'M jostled awake by the sudden slamming of brakes. No telling how long I've been here.

My hands are tied behind me with duct tape soI try to work my hands loose. When that doesn't work, I squirm until my head covering comes off, then kick at the taillights as hard as I can until one breaks, hoping that it's enough for another driver to notice and call the police.

But when the lid of the trunk flies open, I realize my efforts were in vain. The two thugs pull me out of the trunk and toss me to the dirt. They're going to go ahead and kill me now.

Chapter Twenty

Dahlia

I'VE BEEN PUSHED AND PULLED DOWN INTO THE BASEMENT by my struggling attacker, and now the rope around my wrists has been looped and tied to a chair in a dark corner of the basement. My lantern was left overturned upstairs in the struggle, and the only light comes from a pen light gripped between my attacker's teeth, which seems like poor planning to me.

I can hear the person breathing and muttering about some nitwits forgetting to leave the duct tape for her to use. Something about this tells me this was not a well thought out plan to capture and do god-knows-what to me and Blake. Oh god, I hope Blake is OK. I have to fight the lump in my throat and focus on my escape.

"Who's there?" I ask.

A moment passes before a familiar female voice replies. "I suppose it doesn't matter that you know who I am, because you're not getting out of here alive."

I don't know why she's doing this to me, but I know who the voice belongs to.

"Amanda? What in the world?"

"Shut up," she replies coldly. "Where's the money?"

"What money?"

Amanda huffs in exasperation, and in the next moment I feel something cold and metal against my throat. She's not good at tying rope, but she's got a gun, which significantly reduces my chances of getting out of here.

"I should be in Mexico by now. This house was supposed to end up in probate court and the county was going to take possession for back taxes owed. But crazy old Esther had to go fuck it all up because her husband decided to screw us over at the last minute."

The familiar cold snap fills my lungs again, but this time, I don't feel that sense of dread from earlier. Instead, I feel an odd sense of understanding. Either that or I've lost my marbles out of terror.

"Amanda. Put the gun down. You don't have it in you to kill me."

"What I don't have is patience, you stupid girl," she says. "I know Esther figured it all out and must have told you where the money was. Where is it?"

I honestly don't know about any money, but I think my best bet to stay alive is to play along. I close my eyes and try to think what Esther would want me to do right now.

"Esther never told me about any money, but I'm happy to help you find it, Amanda," I say calmly, doing my best to keep my voice from shaking. "Tell me more about it and maybe something will ring a bell for me."

I hear her fidgeting in the dark. In that space of time I realize where I am. I'm sitting on the antique chair in the corner of the basement, and the rope Amanda has used to tie me up is from the noose that had been hanging from the joist. A fresh wave of terror washes over me and I struggle not to hyperventilate.

"If you let me help you, Amanda, you won't have to kill me. I won't breathe a word, I swear."

Finally, she spills it. "John Milton was going to help us. And then he didn't."

"Help you with what?" My fear is starting to subside because I'm dying of curiosity and because she's no longer pressing a gun against my skin. Although, in the dark, I can't see exactly where she's pointing it.

"Mason Construction approached the mayor and me several years back, looking for an incentive not to move out of town. More people were moving into town and commercial taxes were going up to help pave roads, add more emergency services. Mr. Mason didn't like that. He employed six hundred people here at the time, so we knew that we'd lose the election if we let that company go. The council wasn't going to listen to reason about the tax incentives the mayor proposed, so we secretly cut them a deal. We'd make sure they'd win all the city's project bids. We let the company know how low to bid in order to win."

I'm confused. "Lowballing every project in town doesn't seem to be much of a monetary reason to stay put," I say.

Amanda replies, "But cost overruns and change orders add up over time, and pretty soon the city was overpaying for everything. And in return, Mason gave the mayor and me a percentage. Not huge amounts—a little here, a little there. And in order to hide the paper trail, the mayor and I cut in John Milton, too. He was the city finance director at the time, as I'm sure Esther told you. He stowed the money here."

My mind is racing as it processes all of this information. "Here? Literally here in the house?"

"Why do you think I've been so willing to help you organize and plan this ridiculous Fall Festival? Out of the goodness of my heart? No. When that house went to your silly little department, I needed to keep an eye on you."

"I don't understand. You never saw any of the money in all those years?"

"We did, in the beginning. But then John got himself a conscience at some point and stopped. He threatened to go to the police. The only reason he didn't is that he knew it would ruin Esther. Then one day, he just couldn't take it anymore. He went down to the basement and never came back up."

A shiver runs through me. "The rope. The chair. Oh god."

Chapter Twenty-One

Blake

No.

Nobody is going to die tonight. Least of all me. I'm Blake Fucking Pritchard, the most feared and hated bartender in town. And I'm about to fuck people up.

I let go with a massive kick to the chest of the dude closest to me. Not expecting it, he stumbles backward and loses his balance. He's on his ass long enough for me to fight off his partner one-on-one. He's ready to fight off a kick from me, but he's not expecting me to bear down on him head first and take him out at the knees. The brawl continues until the two dudes are groaning on the ground, whimpering like a couple of little bitches.

The duct tape still biting into my wrists, I manage to shimmy one leg and then the other through my arms so that my wrists are now in front of me.

I raise my arms above my head, and then forcefully bring my bound hands down against my middle, the sudden movement spreads my elbows across my ribcage and makes the tape start to give way. I have to do it a number of times, but it works to break the tape and free my hands.

Bloodied and tired and also very confused, I take the keys to the truck and drive like hell.

Chapter Twenty-Two

Dahlia

"BUT WAIT, ESTHER SAID HE DIED OF NATURAL CAUSES."

"Maybe he did," Amanda says, "but once you make someone think she's either losing her mind or her house is haunted, you can make her believe lots of other things, too. The so-called haunting incidents, as well as the chair and the noose, was a nice bit of theater to keep old Esther out of the basement and away from the cache of money, don't you think?"

"But if you know where it is, why do you need me?"

"Because we only took out a little bit at a time. And about half of it has come up missing. Esther is the only explanation. She must have found it and moved it just as we were getting close to being found out. The last finance director got too close to figuring us out; he suspected something was up when he looked at the old books. He was getting real tired of the projects going to the same contractors over and over again, all of them employed by Mason Construction."

My mind hits on something else. This must be why people were quitting left and right from city hall. Either they quit, or maybe they were low-key asked to quit.

"But if she found it, why wouldn't she go to the police? And why wouldn't she have told me about it?"

"Do you think I understand how that batty brain of hers worked?"

I can't stand her talking about my friend like that. Even knowing my anger might get me killed, I blurt out, "You made her that way! You all drove her mad!"

As my anger flares, I hear a loud clank and a rushing wind. When the door at the top of the stairs flies open, a blast of cold air rushes past me and startles Amanda so badly she drops the gun. As it skids across the basement floor, I lunge for it, dragging the chair with me. My hands pull free of the rope and I grab the gun.

The next thing I know, money is raining down all around me. Hundred dollar bills. Thousands of them.

Keeping the gun trained on Amanda, I glance around and see that the cover fell off an old ventilation shaft and the air moving through it is what's causing the money to fly all around us.

I search Amanda's pockets and find her phone, which I use to call the police.

Chapter Twenty-Three

Dahlia

I'm wrapped in a blanket at the police station, trying to convince anyone who will listen to me that Blake is in trouble, when the man himself bursts in the door.

"Oh my god, Blake!" I immediately begin to sob. Ugly, full body sobs.

"D! You're all right. Thank fuck. I drove to the house and you weren't there. I had no idea where you went..."

He's trembling now, almost as badly as I was earlier this morning. I pull the blanket around both of us while reassuring him that I'm fine and not the least bit hurt.

We give our statements to the police, both of us still in shock over what happened tonight. I'm still processing the idea that I had to subdue Amanda Hall, a pillar of the community, and that Mayor Pete is wanted for questioning.

As things wrap up, we learn that John Milton had, over a period of years, stashed away over a quarter of a million dollars in the unused ventilation shafts in the basement of the Milton House.

I let out a shiver and Blake circles his big arms around me. "You're safe, D. I've got you."

I look at him. "But that still doesn't explain the feeling of dread and the coldness. And how did the ventilation shaft just fall open? Do you think maybe Esther's husband was trying to get our attention? Maybe in the afterlife he wanted to make something right?"

Blake kisses me on the forehead. "I may not be convinced of all that afterlife stuff, but I also can't explain some of the things that happened. So I guess...you win the Halloween bet. You've got me at your beck and call, Fall Festival director. For forever." He pecks me on the nose.

"So you actually believe in ghosts?"

"No, I don't. I just want to spend as much time as possible with you."

Epilogue

Fall Festival, one year later

Dahlia

"Oh shit, what does the mayor need now?" I hear my husband say as I clip-clop into the bar in my pumpkin-colored heels.

"The usual, and one more thing," I say, plopping a manila envelope onto the bar.

I'll be honest; it feels pretty good to be mayor. I've spent a whole year dismantling everything the Halls had set up to use our government to benefit themselves, and now it's time to celebrate.

The assets of the former mayor, the mayor's wife, and Mason Construction were all seized during the investigation last year. Unfortunately, the police have never located all of the missing money, and neither have they located the mayor. Everyone's guess is that over the years, he separately squirreled away just what he needed—without telling his wife — with plans to sail off to Mexico with the most recent finance director. People have further extrapolated that he chose to act on Halloween night while his wife hatched her half-assed kidnapping plan, Pete knowing the whole ship was about to sink.

Amanda eventually confessed to getting kickbacks from city construction projects. For years, the city wrote checks for far too large amounts to project managers, who would kick back the difference to the Halls. But the Halls couldn't simply deposit that money in a bank, so Esther's husband had been hiding it at the house for safekeeping.

Just before he died, John grew enough of a conscience to refuse to hand the money over to his partners in crime, but not enough to turn all the money over to the authorities. He stowed all of it in a vent in the basement that he had intended on turning into an apartment to rent out.

After he died, the Halls tried to make Esther think that the house was haunted or that she was losing her mind. Either way, they figured, they'd get her out of the house so they could look for their money.

Now that everyone in town knows the real story, sign-ups for the ghost tour have maxed out. Even though I can't prove or disprove there were ever any ghosts at the Milton House, the Halls' shenanigans have provided the town with enough gossip to make Milton House a popular point of interest. There's even talk of awarding prizes to anyone who can stay overnight there without chickening out. Nobody has taken me up on that bet yet.

I hop up on my knees on the barstool, prop my hands on the bar, and lean over the bar to kiss my husband as he sets down my drink. He pulls me in by the front of my shirt and lays a claiming kiss on my mouth.

"Wearing my shirt again, I see," he murmurs into my mouth, sending shivers down my spine.

"If you don't like it, you should change your wardrobe. Buy yourself less cozy things, like golf shirts."

Blake snorts a laugh and I giggle as we each picture him in a golf shirt.

Popping one button open at my neck, he says, "You got it wrong. I like you in my shirts."

I kiss him again, nibbling his bottom lip playfully. "Then I'll wear them as long as they fit," I say.

He quirks one eyebrow up at me. "Whatever that means, Madam Mayor."

I smile at him and wave the envelope in the air. "Which brings me to the other super-fun game I've invented for this year," I say.

He gestures to the painted jack-o'-lantern. "You mean in addition to everything else you're making me do?"

I sigh and shoot him a knowing smile. "Well, this is a very specific game, only for you."

Blake lolls his head back and looks toward the ceiling as he lists off all of his responsibilities for today. "Let's see. Dunk tank, trick or treating, scavenger hunt, pumpkin pound cake judging, and setting up all the special effects for the ghost tour of the Milton House."

I reach down and grab my drink off the bar and sniff it, wrinkling my nose.

"This again." He shoots one hairy eyeball at me. "It's not watered down. You haven't even tried it."

"Open the envelope," I say.

He mutters but does as I ask. "Like I really have time for one more goddamn Halloween game."

I kiss him on his scruffy chin and the roughness of his angled jaw gives me tingles all down my chest. "I know, baby, but I promise I'll make it worth your while if you just do this one last favor for me, please?"

I trail a line of sloppy, loud smooches down his neck until he growls.

"It better be quick and it better require nothing from me," he says.

"Just open it," I say.

He lets go of me and opens the envelope, pulling out the contents, which includes a piece of paper and another, smaller envelope. He reads what's written on the piece of paper out loud. "It just says 'Positive or Negative?'"

I nod. "You have to guess which one and then turn the page to see if you can open the second envelope."

He grumbles. "All right, fine. Negative."

"Turn the page!"

He does, and reads, "If you guessed negative, go to the clock tower to find your next clue—babe, no. I'm not doing that."

I protest. "But I put clues all over town!"

"Nope," he says. "Changed my mind. I choose positive."

He rips open the second envelope before I can protest, but honestly I'm not even mad.

He looks at the photograph that's inside; it's a picture of a pregnancy test.

"What," he says on a strangely ragged exhale. "What do the double pink lines mean?" Blake's voice goes breathy and trembles, and it's so adorable I want to cry.

"The drink's not watered down, babe. You made it too strong," I say with a wink.

I watch his face as the pieces come into focus. "Holy shit. Are you? Are we...? Are we having a baby?"

I nod as the lump forms in my throat and my voice is choked with tears.

In one swift motion, Blake lifts me up off the barstool and

up over the bar. Before I know what's happening he has me in his arms, my legs wrapped around him. His hands go under my skirt and squeeze my thighs in tight while he kisses me hard.

"When did you find out?" he asks.

"Last week," I say.

"You waited a week! And you've just been walking around in heels and working yourself to exhaustion and making ridiculous games for me to play..."

"I wanted to plan a special surprise for Halloween. You know, to celebrate one year of us getting back together."

His breath shakes as he rests his forehead against my chest. "I'm going to be a dad. We have so much to do. How long do I have to build a nursery, Madam Mayor?"

I smile, thrilled that he's so happy, even though we hadn't actually decided to have kids right away. It just happened. "About seven months. Plenty of time."

Blake's hands, still holding me up by the backs of my thighs, creep up and pet my ass cheeks. I sigh and close my eyes at the delightful scrape of his calloused palms against my skin. My thighs tighten around his middle. He kisses my mouth hard as his hands explore so thoroughly that soon they meet in the middle and spread me open. I gasp, then moan when I feel his finger push aside my panties and sink into my wet heat. Blake roughly whispers into my ear, "I bet we also have time to celebrate before Kenny gets here to open the bar."

"Another bet?" I giggle. "What do I win if we don't both finish in time?"

With one hand, Blake rips away my stretchy lace panties while the fingers inside my sex withdraw to swipe my clit. I grab tight to his shoulders; if he keeps this up, my shaking legs will lose all the strength to hold on to his middle. "Naughty girl. You'd better not bet against me. You'll lose."

I kiss him and nibble on his ears. "As if there's any chance I'd win, with you making me wet as hell."

Blake growls into my breasts, clearly trying to decide whether he his time to work over my nipples. In the end, he leans me against the bar and backs off just enough to reach down between us and unbuckle his belt, the sound of the loosening metal buckle heightening my arousal. I quickly pull out his already throbbing cock. He sucks in a breath at my touch and takes control. With a grunt, he slides his thick, hard length home with a deliciously wet smack, in what might be a record for the shortest amount of foreplay ever.

"Oh my god," I breathe. The feeling of what we do together — my pussy drawing in every inch of his heavy thickness, his movements in me, against me — never fail to make my eyes roll back in my head.

Blake and I have spent plenty of time blowing each other's minds on this bar, behind the bar, in the stock room, on the tables. Doing it slow and gentle, or rough and frenzied. We've had a lot of lost time to make up for.

Just when I'm not so sure his pumping will get the job done for me in time, he plays dirty by moaning against my neck. "You're gonna make that tight pussy come for me whether or not we get caught. You feel so good I'm never pulling out, baby. I don't care who sees us."

"Not fair," I whimper, although I'm past caring about any silly bet. The raw friction of his body against my clit wrecks me in a tidal wave of pleasure. The waves crash over me while his own release surges inside me, both of us crying out in our shared bliss.

As he dots loving kisses up my neck and all over my face, his palm warms my tummy, sending satisfied shivers all over my body.

I kiss him back and weakly say, "I think we both won the bet this time."

. . .

THE END

THANK YOU FOR READING THE HALLOWEEN BET! IF YOU enjoyed it, please consider leaving a review on your preferred site. To check out more books by me, turn the page! And don't forget to sign up for email alerts to be the first to know about my book releases on your favorite book sites.

www.ingramcontent.com/pod-product-compliance
Lightning Source LLC
Chambersburg PA
CBHW051800130726
47987CB00003B/1045